Disney FAIRIES

TinkerBell and the SECRET of the WINGS

PaRRagon

Bath · New York · Cologne · Melbourne · Delhi
Hong Kong · Shenzhen · Singapore

The Winter Woods was the most mysterious place in Pixie Hollow – full of shimmering snowflakes and glistening icicles.

Queen Clarion had made a rule that warm-season fairies weren't allowed to go there. But, one day, curious Tinker Bell jumped across the border! When she landed on the other side, her wings sparkled strangely....

Back at
home, Tink
wanted to know
what had caused
her wings to sparkle.
She wrapped up in her warmest
coat for a trip back to the Winter
Woods. She hid inside a snowflake
basket that was being flown there by an owl.

When she had landed safely in the Winter Woods,
Tink went to the Hall of Winter to find the Keeper
of All Fairy Knowledge, Dewey.
Tink was amazed when she saw him talking to
a winter fairy whose wings were glowing brightly!

Suddenly, Tink's wings
began to sparkle again!
Tinker Bell and the winter fairy,
Periwinkle, looked at each other's
glittering wings in amazement.

Dewey explained that Tink and Peri had been born
of the same laugh – which meant that they were sisters!
The girls couldn't believe it!
"That is why your wings sparkle," Dewey told them.

Tink should have gone straight home to the warm seasons, but Dewey said that she and Peri could spend a little time together first.

So, Peri gave Tink a tour of the Winter Woods. They went for an exciting ride down a frozen waterfall with Peri's friends, Gliss and Spike.

After dark, the Winter Woods got even colder,
so Tink built a fire to keep warm. She told Peri
all about her home.

"I wish I could go there," Peri said. "But I can't live
in warm weather."
"I made it warmer over here ... " replied Tinker Bell.
"Maybe I could make it colder over there."

Just then, the snow floor crumbled beneath them.
The fire was melting it!

A snowy lynx picked up Tink and Peri and took them
back to Dewey, who told Tink that she must return home.

Tinker Bell had an idea. She hugged Peri and whispered,
"Meet me back here tomorrow!"

When Tink arrived back home, she told her friends all about Periwinkle. She also shared her idea with them – a snowmaker! They got straight to work building the machine, which would make it cold enough for Peri to visit Tink.

The next day, they brought the snowmaker to the border. "This is your ticket to the warm side of Pixie Hollow!" Tink told Peri and her friends.

Tucked safely under a snow shower that the snowmaker had made, Periwinkle went on an exciting tour of the warm part of Pixie Hollow.

Then, Peri showed Tink and her friends one of her fairy talents – she coated a flower with glittering frost!

But a little while later, Peri's wings started to wilt. The snowmaker was running out of ice and Peri was getting too warm!

Tink knew she had to rush her sister back to the Winter Woods straight away.

Lord Milori – the Lord of Winter – was waiting for them at the edge of the Winter Woods.

"This is why we do not cross the border," he said. "The rule is there to protect you."

At that moment, Queen Clarion, the queen of Pixie Hollow, arrived. She agreed that the rule was for everyone's safety.

Lord Milori pushed the snowmaker into the icy river as Tink and Peri unhappily hugged goodbye.

Back at home, Queen Clarion tried to help Tinker Bell to understand the rule. She told Tink about a warm-season fairy and a winter fairy who had fallen in love a long time ago. One of the fairies had broken a wing because they had crossed the border – and there was no cure for a broken wing.

As Queen Clarion spoke, Tink looked out of the window and saw something strange – snowflakes were falling!

At the border of the Winter Woods, the snowmaker was stuck at the top of a waterfall. Chunks of ice from the river were pouring into it and it was spraying out snow!

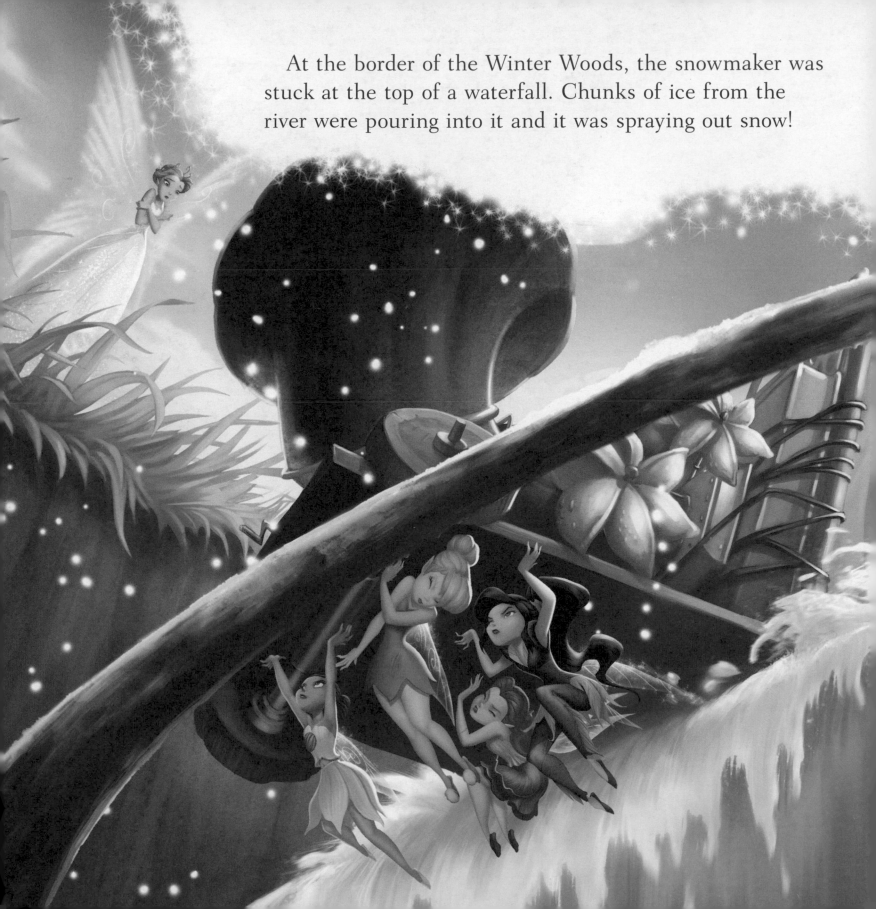

The fairies managed to push the snowmaker out of the waterfall, but it was too late – the seasons had been thrown out of balance.

Everyone was worried – a freeze was now on its way to the warm part of Pixie Hollow. If the Pixie Dust Tree froze, there would be no more pixie dust!

The fairies got straight to work. Some rounded up insects to bring them to shelter ...

... while others rushed to cover the tree with blankets of moss. Would they be able to save it?

Then, Tink remembered the flower that Peri had coated with frost. She flew to the Winter Woods to find her sister.

"I think there's something you can do!" Tink said urgently. "Your frost — it kept the flower alive."

Gliss explained that frost was like a little blanket. It tucked warm air inside — keeping out the cold.

"We could frost the Pixie Dust Tree!" Peri realized.

The winter fairies worked together to quickly frost the Pixie Dust Tree before the freeze hit. After the freeze had passed, the sun came out and melted the ice from the tree. Slowly, the pixie dust started flowing again. The tree was saved!

But Tink realized that she had broken a wing when she had flown back to the Winter Woods. As the sisters said goodbye, an explosion of light burst from their wings. The magic between them healed Tink's wing!

From that day on, warm-season fairies could visit the winter fairies whenever they liked! All they needed was a little frost to keep their wings safe. Tink and Peri would never have to say goodbye again.